NO ANSWER

BY: JASON JOHNSON

"You're trying to escape from your difficulties, and there never is any escape from difficulties, never. They have to be faced and fought."

-Enid Blyton

INDEX

Prologue 5

Chapter 1...10

Chapter 2...17

Chapter 3...23

Chapter 4...29

Chapter 5...34

Chapter 6 41

Epilogue 49

Prologue

The main street in a residential area was busy. On the left side of the street, a little girl came out of the ice cream parlor. The girl was about 9-10 years old; she was wearing a pink dress, her hairs were combed very gently and she also has a candy in her hand.

Then she put the candy in her pocket and got busy on her strawberry cone. She was busy licking as she wasn't aware of what was going to happen. She was strolling and licking her ice cream. A car was coming from behind her at a steady speed and another car was coming from the opposite direction of it. The girl was busy licking but noticed that a car was at high speed, but she continued her licking as the car passes her. There comes the BANG sound at her back. She becomes very frightened by that as she lost the grip of her cone and falls to the ground.

She turns and sees that both the car was banged into each other; she becomes very nervous about that. On the other side, a man comes out of the car and walks to the other car. Another overweight man comes out of the other car.

"Hey, you fucking idiot." says the man in the black shirt.

The overweight man looks very frightened by the other one. He knows that it was his mistake.

"Hey." "Who the fuck are you?"

He knows his mistake as he simultaneously started to apologize.

"I'm sorry." "I'm sorry."

"Are you blind?" "You can't see it's a local street." Says The black shirt, man.

Other people were also starting to gather at the accident location, hoping, no one was injured. As in both of the cars, only a particular one was presented. The overweight man was apologizing to him.

"I'm sorry, mate."

He says with a disappointing look on his face.

"I'll pay the expenses of it."

"Yes." "You'll have to pay for it, and I don't want any excuse."

"Sure, sir."

Other people were thinking that anyone had got injured, but they got to know that situation was under control when they were getting it closer. Two men were talking on the right side about the accident. Both were around the same age in their mid-50s; one of them was very confused.

"What happened here?" asked Man 1.

Man 2 sighs and answers.

"Look at that man…" says Man 2.

He was pointing towards the overweight man; he's the main reason for everything, as everyone was getting it slowly. The man's aggression in the black shirt was genuine because the other one had made a mistake.

"Yes." Says the man 1.

Saying that, Man 1 looks at the other man as he was lighting up his cigarette. Then he replied.

"Yes, that is the reason for it."

"Oh!!!"

"Yes." "He was driving at high speed, and you know what happens when a high-speed car gets out of control.

"Yes."

He nods.

"Does anyone have injury?" asked Man 1.

"No."

He sighs and says.

"There was only one person in each cars." The other nods.

"Okay."

"Yeah, and you are looking at both of them." Says man 1

2.

Again he started to smoke his cigarette while the other man was looking at the accident place. The situation was under control.

"Sophie!!!!" "Sophie......"

The small girl was hearing someone's noise, so she turns towards the other side. A slim lady in her early 30s emerges to her; she has brown hair, clear skin and she's medium height. Tension was on her face as she comes to the girl.

"Sophie!!"

"Mom...."

The lady grabs and hugs her in her arms.

"Baby, are you okay?" asked the lady.

"Yes, mom..."

"I just heard about the accident," says The lady, "I was so worried about you, that's why I came."

"I'm fine, mom."

"Did you get your candies?" asked The lady.

"Yes." Says the girl.

"And what about the ice cream?" asked The lady.

The girl indicates to the ground as the lady looks for it, the strawberry cone was on the ground.

"It slipped from my hand." Says The girl.

"Sweetie." "Don't worry about it; I'll buy a new one for you," says The lady with a satisfied smile.

The smile reveals how much she was worried about her; that's mother's love for her child.

"Come on, honey." "Let's go home." The lady.

"Sure, mom."

They both turned and started walking.

"I love u, baby."

"I love u too, mommy..." She replied with a smile on her face.

Suddenly a black sedan car passed them, it took a right as the board in the side revealed "City Train Station-2 miles". The car races away in that direction at a steady speed. The road was filled with many cars as it was morning and office time.

Chapter 1

A car takes a right cut and drives down the road, a muscular guy was driving the car and his biceps were clearly revealed from his shirt. On the other seat, there was a slim guy with clear skin and a slight beard, he's drinking a can of coke. The muscular one was busy driving as he takes another right. Then he just looks out of the window as his expression was revealing that he had seen something tremendous. He slows down the car to look at it. The other guy notices it and simply had a questionable reaction on his face.

"What happen?" asked The Slim one…

"Look at that."

He looks outside for it; it was a large house with a tremendous structure. The exterior was enough to give a slight impression of the interior, he also admires the house.

"Amazing."

"Yes," said The Muscular guy, "But there is something else."

The bearded guy becomes confused about it. He was wondering what he was saying.

"What else?"

"Do you know?" asked The muscular guy, "Who owns this house?"

The other one replied simultaneously.

"Nope," replied The Slim guy with a gentle smile.

In reply, the muscular one also smiles and looks in-front for driving. The Slim one takes another sip of the coke and asks.

"Tell me. Max." "Who owns it?" The other one smiles and says.

"Benjamin Taylor."

The reaction was enough for anyone to get that he knows him. But his shocker was revealing something different. He looks at him.

"Benjamin Taylor."

"Yes." Replied The muscular guy as he was busy driving the car.

"The Great businessman," says The Slim one… He looks at him as said.

"Yes." The Muscular Guy.

That was enough for the one who wants to know, who Benjamin Taylor was. The Slim guy again drinks the coke, but his face was revealing that he had got to know something curious and unknown. The muscular guy smiles a bit looking at him, then suddenly accelerates the car.

"What happened?"

"No." "Nothing." Says the slim guy "I just…"

Before he can say anything, he was completed by the other one.

"I just got to know that!!" He looks at him.

"Yes," says The Slim Guy.

"I want to be like him," says The muscular one.

"Why?" "Can you just live a normal life?"

"No..."

"Why?" "You know some crime events that happened in the city involves him."

"I want to do something unusual," says The muscular guy, "Something different from others."

The Slim guy shakes his head in amazement. The car took another left and runs down the free and vacant road.

"I know that he is involved, but still, I admire him." "I want to be an entrepreneur like him." The slim one looks at him.

"What?" asked The muscular.

"Jesus Christ, I thought you wanted to follow his bad habits," says The Slim one in relief.

"Come on man," The muscular one, "I just want to learn a good thing." He says.

The other one smiles and says.

"That's the way you should be."

"Yeah..."

"And did you know that there are many of his cases still running in court?"

"What?"

"Exactly."

The main urban area was filled with people on the road and the streets; the buildings were also very big in the main area. The infrastructure was tremendous and well developed, there was also traffic as cars, bicycles, and trucks were also on the road. The lights turn green and the car accelerates down the road, there was also some kind of thugs on the street; they were about 2-3 groups of thugs in the local street areas. A group was near the shop, the group was of three people as they were busy talking with each other, one of the thugs was a tall guy but with a lean physique.

"It's all going bad," says Thug 1.

The second one was having a cigarette as he puffs. But the third one, who a bit short heightened replied.

"Yes, you are right." Says Thug 2.

"Things aren't very easy," says Thug 1.

Simultaneously the third one stops smoking and says.

"What are you guys talking about?" asked Thug 3. "What?" Thug 1.

"I don't find any kind of difficulties." Replied the Thug

3.

The other 2 look very surprised by that.

"What are you talking about?" asked The Thug 2, "The cops are all around and at this time it's very difficult."

The third one smiles and says.

"Why are you guys worrying about it?" asked The Thug

3.

"Why shouldn't we man?" Thug 1.

"The cops are there because of the murders taking place in the area." Thug 2. He says with a pleasant expression on his face.

He looks at Thug 2. As he again smokes and puffs.

"Why you aren't understanding, James?" Thug 2.

"What?"

"This is not the perfect time to hunt." Replied Thug 2.

"Yes," Thug 1, "He is absolutely correct." "Try to understand," says Thug 2.

"Even the other group of thug had stopped their work for few days," says Thug 1.

"Just because of police," says Thug 2.

Thug 3 wasn't saying something. He was silent but was busy puffing his cigarette.

"James…"

He looks at him.

"Are you getting our point?" asked Thug 1.

"Yes," says Thug 3, "Why not?" Thug 1 shakes his head.

"Look," Thug 2, "Look nobody wants to go to jail." "Yes," says Thug 3.

"I said no one," Thug 2.

He nods.

"So please," says Thug 2, "We have to stop for few days."

"Okay, okay." "Don't worry," says Thug 3.

"Yes."

"When things will be alright, we'll again start," says Thug 3.

"Thank god," says Thug 1, "You got it." Thug 3 nods.

"Our today's plan is canceled, but we'll perform on some other day," says Thug 2.

"Sure," says Thug 3, "We are a group and we'll work by our mutual understandings.

"Yes."

All three of them smiles a bit looking at each other, then they started walking, as they pass the grocery shop. The third one was still busy smoking and walking down the street. Some people were busy in the grocery shop as it looked like there had been a sale or kind of that on the products. The second thug noticed the crowd in the shop, he was a bit stunned by that but ignored it. But his fellow mate doesn't… "Have you seen the crowd?" Thug 1.

The first one turns to him and says.

"Yes." "It's unbelievable."

"I mean they don't have any fear of the murders which had happened in the area," says Thug 1.

"No man, Fuck em," says Thug 2, "Those bitches are busy in the sale, doesn't have any fear for death."

The third one was walking a bit ahead of them but was listening to them very carefully. The cigarette was still in his mouth as he was busy puffing, but the other two were busy with their talk.

"Yes," Thug 1, "When it will happen with them, then they'll understand." He says in a heavier voice.

"Leave it, man." "I said na…. Fuck em."

They laugh. But suddenly the smoker says…

"Don't worry guys." "Our robberies will make them afraid of doing their normal activity." Thug 3.

"Yeah, man." Thug 1.

This time all three of them laughs broadly on it.

Chapter 2

L ater the Police cars were on the streets because some severe things were happening in the area, but anyone similarly like thugs, who would be around the street, would definitely not believe that various crimes happened around the area. The people were busy with their lifestyle as they had always been.

Back on to the same grocery shop, but this time it was evening. There were some cars around the street, the sun was about to set. The street was still busy as the cars and bicycles were on and the rush was still on in the shop. People were busy taking advantage of the sale, because not many time grocery shops give sale on a price drop on their products. Simultaneously, two ladies came out of the shop with bags in their hands. The bag was filled with general products.

One of them was in her early 30s, she was tall and slim with clear skin and black hair. The other one was medium heightened with brown hairs, she looks in her early 40she was slightly overweighted. But her bag was also filled more than the other one, they both were smiling and busy talking with each other. Their smile was enough to reveal that their happiness was because of what they had earned in the sale.

"You could have taken more."

"I thought this could be enough," says The tall one.

The other lady laughs at this.

"Come on, Anna." She says with a smile.

But the other one didn't reply to it as she was simply smiling and walking.

"You should know about it that price drop on these kinds of shops is very rare," says The overweighted lady.

The other one replied with a nod and a smile.

"I can understand that you are newly married, but as a housewife, you have to understand these kinds of things." They both laugh at it.

"Yes." "I'm less experienced as compare to you," says The tall lady.

The other one laughs and says.

"And yes, you have to interact with more people around the street," says The overweighted lady.

"Okay," says the tall one, "I'm getting it."

"I know that you are new to this area, but you have to interact."

She nods.

"And don't worry," She says with a smile, "I'll help you to introduce among the others."

"Thank you so much," says The tall one.

The other lady looks at her with surprise.

"Hey......" "We are friends, Anna." She smiles and says.

"Yes."

The overweighted one smiles and nods.

"From how many years have you been living here?" asked The tall one with a gentle smile.

"Ummm." "For around 20 years."

"20."

"Yes."

"Pretty long," says The tall one, "That's why you are experienced."

Both of them laugh.

"I'm more experienced than you in many ways," says The Over weighted one with a smile.

They both look at her and burst out of laugh.

"I got it." The tall one.

"You should," says The over-weighted one.

"Yes." Says The tall one.

"But Anna," says The other one, "This place is pretty more than it looks."

The tall one was noticing her very carefully.

"Some says that it's not safe and all," says The overweighted one, "But it's not like that."

"Yes, even I believe that." "I know that things that are happening from the last few weeks are terrible, but I hope that it will be fine."

"Anna, it's a great place." "And people are also very gentle and helpful."

The other one nods.

"So, you don't have to worry," says The overweighted lady, "You have chosen a great place to live." She smiles.

"So when you planning for a baby." Anna is shy a bit but replied.

"Come on," says the tall one.

Both of the ladies smiled and continued their walk. Finally, they took a left down the road.

The inside the store was big with lots and lots of different kinds of products were in it. Elijah was very tired as his eyes were revealing it. He was in his mid-20s as he was standing with extremely clean uniform stocks on the tall shelves inside that bustling store. He was busy with his work. A Customer approached with a frown written on his face and a bag full of regretful purchases in his arms.

"Yo, you. I wanna' return these." Customer.

Elijah looked towards him and forced a genuine-looking smile.

"Yeah, no problem. Let me take you to the customer service desk," said Elijah.

He shook his head.

"Nah, there's a line there. Do it at one of the tills." Customer.

"I'm sorry, but we can only process returns at the customer..."

"That's bullshit."

"I'm sorry sir, but that's store policy."

"My cousin works at a place like this; he says any of you can do the returns."

"Sorry, but that's not the case here." Elijah.

"You're an idiot."

"Excuse me?"

"Deaf, too." Customer.

Elijah sighs.

"Sir, I'm just trying to help you the best I can," says Elijah.

The customer was getting very aggressive as his voice was getting very high.

"No, you're fuckin' not. You're being fuckin' incompetent." Customer.

This time Elijah shook his head. Then says…

"I'm sorry, I don't know what you want me to do."

He pokes Elijah's chest.

"Return my fuckin' stuff." Customer.

"I already told you, I can't." Elijah.

"I don't know what I expect. Of course, the stupidest people work in shit jobs like this. I bet your mom is fuckin' proud," says Customer.

The customer walked away and down the aisle to harass somebody else, Elijah was staring to the ground. After taking a few calming breaths, he eventually continued stacking the shelves. Micheal, who was in his late 30s emerged. With face cold as stone, the balding boss drags a large stocking trolley into the aisle, as he stopped in front of the angry customer.

"Can you fuckin' help me?" Customer.

He nods.

"I'll certainly try; what do you need?" asked Micheal.

"I need to return this shit, but the line's too long. I'm in a hurry."

"Sure thing, I'll just get Elijah to open up a new till for you."

He beckons Elijah over.

"Him? Really? He said he couldn't do shit," says Customer.

Elijah hesitated but made his way over to both of them. The boss asked when Elijah came.

"Is it true you didn't want to help this gentleman?" Micheal.

He replied.

"Well, Mr. Garner, during training, we were told that," says Elijah.

"You should look after customers to the best of your ability." Micheal.

"This guy gets it." Customer.

"Perhaps we need to revisit your training," says Micheal.

"I'm sorry, Mr. Garner." Elijah.

"Please help this gentleman with his returns."

Elijah nodded and led the customer out of the aisle and towards the tills.

"You're lucky you ain't getting fired."

Chapter 3

Later Elijah hands the customer's card and receipt back. "Have a good day." Elijah.

The customer snatched them without saying anything. Then with a shake of his head, he leaves. He passed Sasha; Sasha was around 18 as she was dressed in the same uniform as Elijah, but much less scrupulous. The customer grins and runs his hand across her ass; she flinched and moved back.

He laughed and then left the store.

After catching her breath, she spotted Elijah looking a bit downtrodden. Then she made her way to him.

"What's wrong, E?" asked Sasha.

Elijah looked at her and asked.

"Do you know him?" Elijah.

"The guy that just groped my ass? Hell no." He shook his head.

"Just another creep that thinks he can have whatever he touches." Sasha.

"Makes me sick."

She sighs and asked.

"He didn't grab your ass, did he?"

"No, he just turned Mr. Garner against me." "What do you mean?" Sasha asked.

"I was told it's against protocol to open up a new till to do a return."

She nods and says...

"Yeah, it's supposed to be done at the desk." Sasha says.

"Well, Mr. Garner made me do it."

"You know him, always trying to keep the customers happy," says Sasha.

"But I already told the customer that it couldn't be done.

I look like an idiot. I feel like an idiot."

"Okay, that's a dick move."

Then simultaneously, she spotted Micheal approaching. "Speak of the devil, catch you later." Sasha.

She left as Micheal came opposite Elijah. As he asked.

"Mr. Garner, what we did goes against the training." He asked.

Then he replied in deep voice.

"No, what's against training is telling the customer you can't do something that you can." Micheal.

"But I didn't think we were supposed to?" He says, shaking his head.

"Look, I'll make it easy for you, pal. Next time anything like this comes up, just ask me, alright?" asked Micheal.

Elijah nodded.

"Now, could you make this up to me by covering

Randy's shift."

"Tonight?" Elijah questioned.

"Yeah, come on, I need you, Elijah." Micheal.

"Okay, yeah." He says.

"Brilliant, glad to see you're one of the team." Micheal.

He pats Elijah on the shoulder.

"Keep up the good work."

Micheal left him with his thoughts as he was staring dead-eyed at the cold white walls ahead of him.

Inside the small and unremarkable room as this was the staffroom of the grocery store, Elijah takes a few moments to organize his thoughts. Struggling to continue working late into the night, he sips a cup of water. Suddenly his phone buzzes. He took out his phone and looked at the screen, it was of Ebony; he takes the call.

"Baby, where are you?" Ebony.

"I'm still at work." He replied.

"What, why?"

"Mr. Garner needed me to cover a shift." Elijah.

"But what about Aaliyah? You're supposed to be taking me to her house like, right now." He downs his head.

"I'm sorry, Eb, but I can't tonight."

"Of course, you're puttin' yourself first, like always." "I didn't have a choice." Elijah.

"Oh, you never have a choice, do you? Maybe it's time you grew some fuckin' balls." Ebony.

"No, I messed up earlier, so I couldn't say no."

"Whatever Elijah. People know they can just walk all over you and like, screw the both of us over."

"That's not true, Ebony."

"Then why are you still at the store?" Ebony replies.

"You wouldn't get it." Elijah says.

"What's that supposed to mean?"

Elijah was busy in his talk with Ebony. Suddenly he heard something. Still on the call, he looked towards it.

"Get off me!" Screams Sasha...

After recognizing Sasha, he rushed towards the front of the store where she was. On the other side, the call was still connected.

"You don't give a shit about anything I want. Ever! I'm sick of coming second." Ebony.

"I've got to go." Elijah.

"What? Elijah, I'm talking to you!"

Near the billing area of the store, the customer from earlier was standing intimidatingly close to Sasha. He moved with a drunken sway.

"What's wrong, sweetie?"

Sasha had a horror look on her face. She was getting the intensions of him.

26

"I said no!" Sasha exclaimed.

Finally, Elijah stormed up to them. He looked towards them,

"What's the problem?" Elijah.

The customer looked at him and says... "Oh, not you, again." Says the drunk customer.

"You're drunk, sir; I think you should leave." Elijah.

Again he shouted.

"Fuck no! This slut is being a bitch."

"Please don't talk to her like that."

"He grabbed my ass again!" Sasha says.

"Please, sir, just go."

"Oh, come on, you were asking for it." Says the drunk man.

First time Elijah raised his voice.

"Stop, before I have to throw you out!"

"Oh, now who's a big boy? Buddy, I'm not leaving, and what the fuck are you gonna' do about it?"

"Please, just go." Elijah.

"No."

The customer wrapped his arm around Sasha's waist and pulled her close to him. Then Elijah got in between them and pushed them apart. In response, the man pushed Elijah back hard.

"Get your fucking dirty hands off me!"

He grabbed Sasha's arm, but Elijah pushed him away again. The customer threw a punch that sent Elijah to the ground. He stood soon after and took his own swing that connects with the customer's jaw.

"No! Elijah, stop!" Elijah.

The customer hits the ground, nose bloody. He slowly gets up and backs up towards the door.

"Don't you know who I am? You're fucked buddy! You're fucked!"

He left the store. Then Sasha puts her hand on Elijah's arm as they both took catch their breath.

"Are you okay?" Elijah asked.

She nodded.

"Me? I'm fine. Are you okay?" Sasha.

Elijah wiped the blood off his face, then he nodded slowly, Sasha sighs. They both were silent as they were remembering what all just had happened. Elijah had his head down.

Chapter 4

ater Elijah leaves the glass doors of the store behind him. His eyes revealed his mood, he was very tired and exhausted; then he took his phone out and searches for the contact of his mother. Finally, he founds and taps on it, putting the phone to his ear, he waits, but there's no answer. Fighting to keep the tears from falling, he drops the phone; pain was in his eyes but continued his long journey home.

Finally, Elijah entered his tiny but methodically clean apartment. He was lost somewhere, he almost trips as his foot meets a large box of memories long thought lost.

"Your mom left that shit for you."

Elijah kneels by the box and goes through his old childhood objects.

"She was here?" Elijah.

A girl emerged, she was in her early 20s. She was Ebony, with more time and money spent on her face and hair than anything else around her. She was dressed casually as she comes and leaned on the wall.

"She said that's the last bit of your life she had left and that she doesn't want you bothering her again." Ebony. He clutched a once dear action figure in his hands.

"So are you taking me to Aaliyah's or what?"

He didn't hear her and just continued to stare at his mother's parting gift.

"Hello? I'm talking to you!" Ebony.

Then he asked.

"What?"

"Aaliyah's?"

"Eb, I'm tired."

"I don't give a shit; you said you'd take me."

"It's all the way 'cross town; I don't wanna' drive no more tonight."

"You said you would take me, don't fuckin' lie. You're a goddamned liar!" Ebony.

"Please, just give me one night without you tearing into me."

"Ain't nobody tearing into you. Keep your fucking word. You said you'd take me, so take me!"

"I'm sorry, I didn't know I'd have to work extra

tonight."

"Not my problem."

He slowly puts the action figure down.

"Just let me change, then we'll go."

"Oh my god. Don't take all day." Ebony says.

Elijah picked up the box and entered his bedroom. She stood alone in the main room, shaking her head for a moment.

"Idiot."

Not many cars were on the street as it was late at night. Some people were busy at the bakery shop and some were busy in the grocery one. Some kids were busy walking with their parents as they had candy in their hands. Their smile was revealing their happiness. There was a restaurant on the left side of the street as there were some cars and bicycle, parked outside of it. Things were very calm as a car passed the restaurant at medium speed, it was of Elijah's.

Finally, Elijah's car stopped outside Aaliyah's shabby apartment. Ebony opened the door and left without a word, he watch her as she entered the apartment building and disappeared out of sight. Hesitantly, he took out his phone and called his mom again, but there's no answer. Gripping the wheel tightly, he took a few moments before driving off to his next destination.

Later Elijah was sitting alone on a cold bench in an otherwise picturesque park. His face looked dull and helpless. He was staring ahead, fiddling with the phone in his hands, he turned the phone over and flicked through pictures from happier days. He stopped on one of him and his very young son. They both grin at the camera, happiness captured forever in that perfect frame. The screen changed suddenly - Sasha's calling. Elijah looked and then answered.

"Sorry, E, I wiped out. What's up?" Sasha says.

"Just wanted to see if you wanted to hang out?"

"Right now?" Sasha replied

"Yeah." Said Elijah.

"Oh, sorry, it's late and I'm really tired."

"Yeah, that's cool, I know how it be." Elijah.

"Everything alright with you, though? How's your jaw?"

31

"It's fine. I'm just happy you're okay."

"I owe you, E."

"Don't sweat. But yeah, we'll catch up later." Elijah said.

"See you at work." Sasha replied.

Sasha ends the call, Elijah lowered the phone and continued staring into the distance. He was silent as he sat there alone. The tears surge from his eyes and he quickly wipes them and walks back to his car.

Like the rest of the apartment, Elijah's bedroom was small and spotless. He wakes up alone, it's clear Ebony didn't return home last night; he stood up, and then immediately makes the bed. Suddenly his phone started to

buzz. He's had several missed calls from Stacy, he looked at it and sighs, then he called her.

"Oh, I see, so you're ignoring me now?" Stacy.

"No, sorry, I had a long day yesterday. I only just got up." Elijah.

"Just got up? I didn't realize you were lazy as well."

He shook his head.

"What do you need, Stacy?"

"You don't even know what's wrong? Where's your money, Elijah? Do you want your son to starve or something?" says Stacy.

After listening to her, he was a bit confused, what she was saying.

"It's not due yet."

"Yes, it is." Stacy replies.

"No, we agreed I'd send it on the 14th of each month. That's around when I get my check."

"You paid me on the 5th last month." Stacy.

"You said you needed it early."

"I did. But now I need it early, again. Why don't we simplify this and make that the deadline each month?" Elijah was getting annoyed by her statement.

"I can't; I only get paid around the 14th, that's why we agreed to that date." Elijah.

"Stop making things difficult, Elijah. Stop making excuses not to support your kid?"

"That's not it."

"Listen, if I don't get the money by the end of the week, this won't look good for any future custody hearings. Do you understand? If you want to keep seeing Malik, you'll pay what you owe when I need it."

"Stacy, please, don't do this." He said.

"I didn't do shit Elijah, you did this. Get my money."

"Stacy..."

The call disconnected. He stands frozen in the

room.

Fighting tears from falling from his eyes, thinking of the fact that he may never see his child again.

Chapter 5

Later Elijah forced a smile behind the checkout counter. His uniform was subtly disheveled. He scanned a few miscellaneous items for a smiling customer.

"And that'll be $32.18, please." Elijah says.

The customer swiped their card and took the bags.

"Have a good day."

The customer smiled and walked. Suddenly Micheal approached.

"Elijah, a word?"

Elijah followed him away from the counter, they both walked towards the staffroom. Elijah was very confused by Micheal's behavior. In the small back room, Elijah and Micheal entered; the room was very neat and clean as there wasn't anyone else. He motioned to a seat, Elijah nodded and sits.

"What happened last night?" Micheal asks.

Elijah was surprised by the question, but he replied immediately.

"A customer assaulted Sasha."

"And you responded to that by punching him?" Michael says.

"He tried to hurt her."

"Elijah, he's made a statement to corporate."

"I'm sorry, Mr. Garner."

"It doesn't matter if you're sorry; it doesn't change the fact that you lashed out at a customer." Micheal.

Elijah stared at the floor.

"His dad is a lawyer, and he's threatened to make heads roll unless I let you go"

He looked at Micheal in shock.

"No, Mr. Garner, I'll do whatever you need to fix it; please don't fire me."

"I'm sorry, Elijah, but I've got no choice."

"Mr. Garner, you can't…"

"Please don't make a fuss."

"I'll do anything, Mr. Garner, please."

"I'm sorry, but you've got to go." Micheal.

Elijah was shocked as he was trembling. He wasn't able to do anything as he was lost in Micheal's word.

"Elijah…"

Elijah didn't speak anything, he simply unclips and hands over his nametag. He stood and looked at Micheal for a moment, but again, without saying anything, he leaves the room, his head was down as he came out. Tears were continuously falling from his eyes, his hopes were destroyed as he walks down the store.

Elijah was walking all alone on the street, not a single person was around the street, it was cold too. Elijah had his head covered with a hoodie as he continued his walk, his head was still down. Suddenly a car passes by him; it was a red color BMW, the open BMW had 3 girls and a boy who was driving. Loud music was on as they were shouting and smiling. Elijah looked at the boy as the girls were looking at him. Smiles all around as they drive down the road. Elijah stopped for a moment as he watches them go out of his sight.

Later Elijah entered his home, cheeks wet, head was still down.

"Ebony?"

When he realized she's not home, he took his phone out and called her. She wasn't picking it up, again he started to sob. He was about to move as his phone beeps; he looked at it, it was a text from Ebony.

"What?"

He replied.

"Where r u?"

She responded: "At Aaliyah's won't be home tonite".

He lowered his phone and sighs, then he made his way to the bedroom. He was getting continuous disappointment from Ebony and this was very tough for him.

Later Elijah was in his bedroom as he pulls out the box of his childhood things from beside the bed and fingers through them, tears dripping down slowly. He picked up a

CD with a hastily scrawled title that revealed "Elijah's Mix"; he turned on the practically ancient stereo at the corner of the room and put the CD in and hits play. Sitting on the floor as the songs from his childhood wash around him, he closed his eyes and began imagining the good times. He remembered when he still had hope that all of this would work out, it stirs him to call his mom without hesitation; but there's again no reply.

While on the phone, he sent a text to Sasha. He types... "Ready when u r".

Then waits patiently for a reply that never comes.

Time passed as it was late at night. Still sitting on the floor, the last song of the CD comes to an end; his eyes were tired and glassy as he was staring dead ahead. His phone buzzed and with excitement, he grabbed it to find a text from his mom. He smiles as it was a hope for him, but it was destroyed when he opens it.

"Stop calling me."

He dropped his phone to the ground as the fountain of tears flow, he suddenly lunges for a box under the bed; his whole body shook as he pulls it out slightly before getting second thoughts and thrusting it back to where it belongs. Collapsing to the ground, he sobs uncontrollably until he falls asleep.

In the morning, Ebony entered the bedroom to find Elijah asleep on the floor. She kneels by him and puts her hand on his shoulder. "Elijah?" Ebony.

He woke up slowly, his whole body willing him to stay on the floor.

"What happened?" Ebony.

He shrugs.

"Tell me." Ebony.

"You don't care." Elijah.

"We don't know until you tell me." Ebony.

"It'll just make you hate me more."

"I don't hate you, babe."

"You act like you do."

"Well, I don't mean to."

"I don't think you understand that you're the best thing that's happened to me since Malik was born, and I know I don't say it enough, but I really do love you. You're everything to me."

He hugs her tight, but she didn't really hug back.

"I know…" Ebony says…

"Can we just hang out together today? Just you and me?"

"I've got plans, babe."

"And you can't cancel them?"

"No…"

His eyes drifted away from hers.

"Why were you sleeping on the floor?" Ebony.

"I didn't mean to." Elijah.

"What happened?" Ebony.

"I got fired." Elijah.

"You got fired?" He nodded.

"How?"

"A drunk guy attacked Sasha and I punched him."

"You punched him?" He nods.

"When I said to grow some balls, that's not what I meant."
Ebony.

"He was gonna' hurt her." Elijah.

"So? You shouldn't throw your job away for her. That little slut has it coming."

"No, she doesn't." Elijah.

"Oh come on, you've seen the way she looks at every, like, every guy."

"She's not like that."

"You would know."

"Yeah, I would." Elijah.

"And only you of all people could get fired from that shitty job."

"I knew you'd say that." Elijah.

"So, what are you gonna' do now?"

"Stacy said that if I don't pay her this month's money by the end of the week, she'll never let me see Malik again." Elijah.

"She can't do that." Ebony.

"She'll find a way." Elijah.

"Only if you let her. Why don't you use this newfound confidence. That feeling when you punched that guy? Remember it and stop her walking all over us for once." Ebony.

"You think I should see her?" Elijah.

"Yeah, that's a good idea. She'll be nicer if Malik's around." Ebony.

"I doubt it." Elijah.

"Clean yourself up, then go over there and make it clear that you're not gonna' put up with her crap no more. Then, while you're feeling fiery, go back to the store and get your job back."

He downs his head in disappointment.

"I don't think they'll listen to me."

"They might, so long as you don't cry like a little baby." Ebony.

He hugs her again.

"Thank you." Elijah.

She stood and left the room. He dries his eyes.

Chapter 6

It wasn't a very well-maintained apartment and wasn't very big, but bigger than Elijah's one. Here the things were looking very well planned and managed but not so attractive. The living room was filled with many messier things, which would make someone feel down; a girl in her mid-20s emerged. She was Stacy, she heard the bell as she walk towards the door with a face that's used to being displeased and eyes that judge all that you do. Finally, she opened the door, he was none other than Elijah, she allows Elijah into the room.

"You've got some guts coming around here without money." Stacy.

"I thought it would be best to talk face-to-face." Elijah.

"Shouldn't you be at work?"

"They fired me."

She was surprised.

"Please tell me you're joking."

"No, but don't worry, I'm going to convince them to get a job back."

"You couldn't convince a fish back into the water." He looked confident.

"I can, unlike you, Ebony actually believes in me, and she said I could do it." Elijah.

"So when you don't get the job back and when you can't give me the money you owe, what the heck happens then?"

"It's not gonna' happen." "You're an idiot." Stacy.

"I don't care what you think no more, Stacy." Elijah.

"Then you won't care when you never see Malik again."

"Stop saying that! You can't use our son against me." She was getting furious.

"Can't I?"

"Where is he?"

And now she became more aggressive.

"That'll cost you."

"I need to see him."

"Elijah!"

Elijah barged past Stacy, his face lights up as soon as he entered through the living room door and saw Malik, who was just a year old. His bright eyes were wide, with a happy face shining light all around.

"Aw, my boy, I'm so sorry I've been away." Elijah.

He grins as he scoops his son into his arms and holds him close. he giggles.

"Every time I see you, you're bigger and bigger."

Stacy watches them with her arms crossed. He laughed with his child.

"You can't stay for long." Stacy.

"Please, just an hour or so." Elijah.

She shook her head.

"Please, Stacy."

"No."

"You really gonna' do this in front of him?"

"We don't have to."

"What do you mean?"

"You can put her back down and walk out and pretend everything is fine."

"Or?"

"We're going to blow up into a big fight." Stacy.

He looked to his son with eyes torn by sorrow, he nodded and kissed Malik on the forehead before putting him on the floor.

"I love you, my boy." Elijah.

He kisses him again.

"This is hard for me, as well, you know?" Stacy.

"Like hell it is." Elijah.

"I don't like fighting with you. But you've got obligations for your child and I think you're slipping." "I don't believe that," says Elijah, "I'm trying my best." "But your best isn't good enough." Stacy.

"So what am I supposed to do? If I could do anything to make this right, what would it be?"

"I don't know."

"So how the hell am I supposed to?" Elijah.

"Please just go, Elijah." Stacy.

Elijah walked past her again and opened the apartment door.

"You'll see." Elijah.

"What?" Stacy.

"I'm gonna' get this job back, and then I'm going to get full custody of Malik." Elijah.

"No, you won't."

"You'll see." Elijah.

"Get out," Stacy shouts.

"You'll be begging to see him at my door."

"I said get out."

"And I'll let you see him. Because I'm not a fucking monster."

"Get the hell out of my house!" Stacy.

"You've still got time to change it."

"I hope I never see you again."

She pushed him out and slammed the door shut. He sobs as he leaned his head against her door.

Later inside a silent room, Elijah was sitting opposite Micheal.

"Thank you, Mr. Garner, for seeing me again; I know you don't owe me anything." Elijah.

"I can't make this any clearer for you, Elijah." Micheal.

Elijah says with hope in his eyes.

"There's got to be another solution here. I need this job."

"My hands are tied, pal."

"No, you must be able to do something. Would it help to explain my situation?"

"It'll just make it harder for me."

"My ex needs money for our kid and she's not gonna' let me see him again if I can't pay up." "Listen, Elijah. Please, listen carefully. I don't have a choice. I can't let you back." Micheal.

"Please, Mr. Garner, please, I need this. I'll do anything.

I'll work 12-hour shifts. I'll do some free labor. Please, Mr.

Garner, please."

"I'm sorry."

Micheal stood up.

"No, no, please, please, please." Elijah.

"Stop." Micheal.

Elijah started sobbing, he fell to his knees and holds Micheal's hand.

"Please, I've not got much left. If I can't get this job back, I'm not sure what will happen..."

"Just stop, Elijah. You're making a fool of yourself."

"Don't do this!"

Micheal moved back and broke Elijah's grip.

"You need to leave."

Tears fall as he denied.

"No, no, no, please."

"Keep going and I'll have you thrown out. I'll have you banned from here for life; just go." Micheal.

"Mr. Garner..."

"Just go, Elijah."

Elijah eventually stood up and stormed out of the room after a few hesitant moments, tears still streaming. Elijah stormed towards the glass doors and caught Sasha's eye, she smiles at him, but he just turned away and leaves.

Elijah was on the stairs as his tears were unstoppable, he had confidence in him, he had hope, but everything disappeared. Finally, Elijah entered his home; still, tears were falling from his eyes, he kept his shoes on as he walked towards the bedroom; he paused when he heard the sounds of soft moans coming from inside along with music from his childhood CD mix.

He bursts open the door to caught Ebony in the throw of passion under the bedsheets with Deion. A tall and muscular guy in his late 20s. Both of them get shocked to see him.

"Oh my god!" Ebony.

"Oh shit." Deion.

Elijah clenched his fist.

"I'm so sorry, babe, I..." "Why?" Elijah.

"Hey, buddy, listen..." "Shut up!" He shouts.

Then he looked at her.

"Why, Ebony? Why would you do this to me?" Elijah.

"I'm so sorry." Ebony.

"No, you're not. All I ever hear is "I'm sorry" this, "I'm sorry" that. None of you are ever sorry!"

"Don't do anything stupid, buddy…" Deion.

"I told you to shut the fuck up!" Elijah.

Elijah took heavy breaths as Deion and Ebony were standing in tension out of the sheets.

"Get out." Elijah.

She gets surprised.

"What?"

"You want to fuck? I don't care! Just get the fuck out!"

"Baby…"

"Get the fuck out, now!"

Elijah threw his stereo onto the floor; the music dies into a mighty crash. Deion took Ebony's hand and sheepishly left the room, closing the door behind them. After a few moments, Elijah's rage turned to sorrow.

He collapsed, crying out and slamming his fist into the floor. His hands shaking, he called Sasha, but there's no reply. He tried to catch his breath as he slowly takes out the box from under the bed again, he takes the lid off the top to reveal a handgun inside. Whole-body shaking, he called his mom. But as always, there's no reply. He dropped the phone onto the floor and opened a box of ammo and loaded a single bullet into the handgun clip.

He slides the magazine into the handgun with labored breaths and cocked it, sliding the safety off. He tried to steady his breath as he placed the muzzle of the gun against his temple, tears still dripped onto the floor as his finger moved to the trigger. He closed his eyes tightly and squeezed them. He fires the gun and killed himself. The room fells silent for a few moments before his blood-spattered phone began ringing. The call was from his mom, but this time, he didn't answer.

Epilogue

A man in his mid-40s was checking the things in the living room, he was dressed in a police uniform. He moved to the other room, where Elijah's lifeless body was lying on the floor. The blood splash was all over the room, there were two more policemen as one of them was checking the gun. The other one was investigating the bedroom. Then the second policeman says…

"Suicide."

The other one turns and said.

"Certainly."

The officer in his mid-40s was standing at the door when a heard footsteps, which was coming towards them. A woman in her late 40s came and stopped at the bedroom door, she was stunned looking at the lifeless body of Elijah. All three policemen looked at her; tears began to fall from her eyes. She was continuously looking at the body.

"Excuse me?" Says the police, who was in his mid-40s.

She didn't look at him nor responded anything.

"Ma'am." Says the other one.

"You're?"

Finally, her lips moved a bit and the voice came out from her.

"Mother."